Dear Parents:

Congratulations! Your child is taking the first steps on an exciting journey. The destination? Independent reading!

STEP INTO READING® will help your child get there. The program offers five steps to reading success. Each step includes fun stories and colorful art or photographs. In addition to original fiction and books with favorite characters, there are Step into Reading Non-Fiction Readers, Phonics Readers and Boxed Sets, Sticker Readers, and Comic Readers—a complete literacy program with something to interest every child.

Learning to Read, Step by Step!

Ready to Read   Preschool–Kindergarten
• big type and easy words • rhyme and rhythm • picture clues
For children who know the alphabet and are eager to begin reading.

Reading with Help   Preschool–Grade 1
• basic vocabulary • short sentences • simple stories
For children who recognize familiar words and sound out new words with help.

Reading on Your Own   Grades 1–3
• engaging characters • easy-to-follow plots • popular topics
For children who are ready to read on their own.

Reading Paragraphs   Grades 2–3
• challenging vocabulary • short paragraphs • exciting stories
For newly independent readers who read simple sentences with confidence.

Ready for Chapters   Grades 2–4
• chapters • longer paragraphs • full-color art
For children who want to take the plunge into chapter books but still like colorful pictures.

STEP INTO READING® is designed to give every child a successful reading experience. The grade levels are only guides; children will progress through the steps at their own speed, developing confidence in their reading. The F&P Text Level on the back cover serves as another tool to help you choose the right book for your child.

Remember, a lifetime love of reading starts with a single step!

Visit us on the Web!
StepIntoReading.com
randomhousekids.com

Educators and librarians, for a variety of teaching tools, visit us at
RHTeachersLibrarians.com

Library of Congress Cataloging-in-Publication Data
Redbank, Tennant.
The saggy baggy elephant / by Tennant Redbank ; illustrated by Garva Hathi.
 pages cm. — (Step into reading. Step 1, ready to read)
"Adapted from the beloved Little Golden Book, written by Kathryn and Byron Jackson and illustrated by Gustaf Tenggren."
Summary: Sooki the elephant, who has never seen another animal like himself, tries to shrink his saggy wrinkly skin.
ISBN 978-0-553-53588-4 (pb) — ISBN 978-0-553-53589-1 (glb) — ISBN 978-0-553-53633-1 (ebk)
[1. Elephants—Fiction. 2. Self-acceptance—Fiction. 3. Jungle animals—Fiction.]
I. Hathi, Garva, illustrator. II. Jackson, Kathryn. Saggy baggy elephant. III. Title.
PZ7.R24455Sag 2016
[E]—dc23
2014047143

Printed in the United States of America
10 9 8 7 6 5 4 3 2 1

This book has been officially leveled by using the F&P Text Level Gradient™ Leveling System.

THE SAGGY BAGGY
ELEPHANT

Adapted from the beloved Little Golden Book written by
Kathryn and Byron Jackson and illustrated by Gustaf Tenggren

By Tennant Redbank

Illustrated by Garva Hathi

Random House 🏠 New York

4

Sooki dances.
Happy elephant!

One. Two. Three.
STOMP!
The jungle shakes.

One. Two. Three.
KICK!
A tree falls.

A parrot sees Sooki
and giggles.

He teases Sooki about
his saggy, baggy skin.

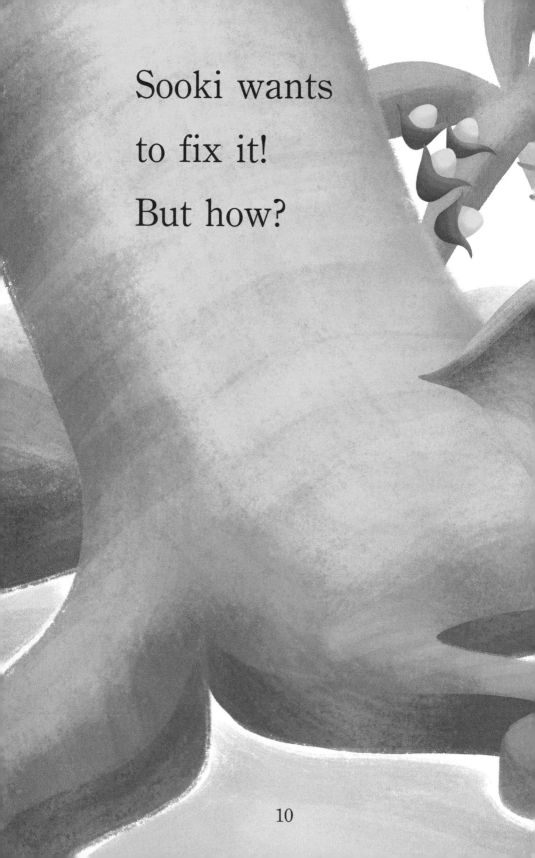

Sooki wants
to fix it!
But how?

Here comes a tiger.

He is not saggy.

Why?
He stays fit!

So Sooki walks.

Sooki rolls.

But his skin is
still too big!

Maybe water will
shrink his skin.

Oh, no!

Here comes a crocodile!

Run!

Sooki finds
a dark cave.

Hide inside, Sooki.

Hide your saggy skin.

Hide your baggy skin.

GROWL.

Here comes a lion.

The lion is hungry.

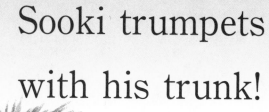

Sooki trumpets with his trunk!

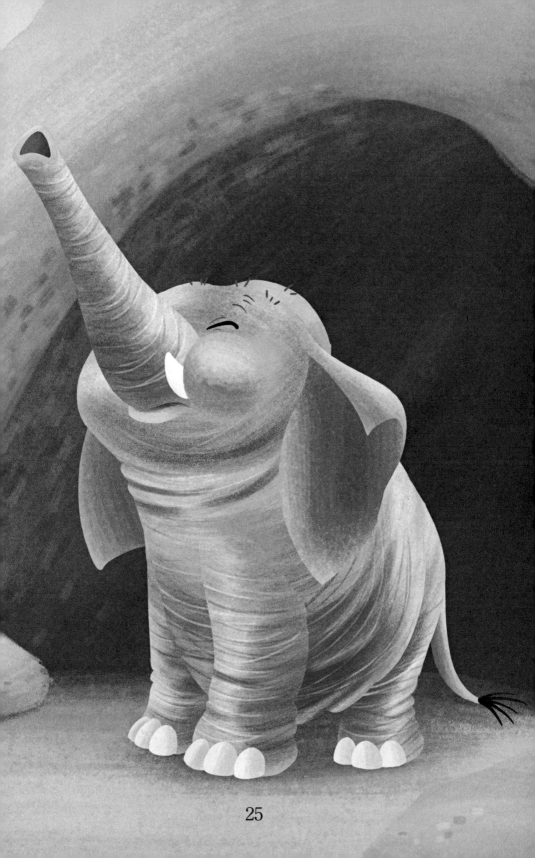

STOMP! STOMP!
Here come
many elephants!

The lion runs away.

Sooki looks
at the elephants.

They have saggy skin.

They have baggy skin.

Just like him.

Sooki dances.

The elephants dance.

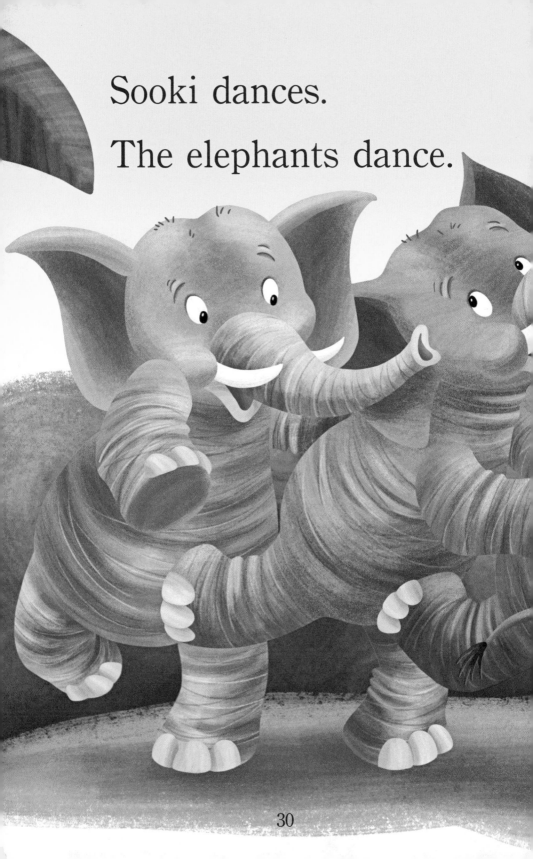

One. Two. Three.
KICK!

Happy elephants.